QUIRKY TIMES AT QUAGMIRE CASTLE

Life couldn't be worse for Jack and Emily.
Quagmire Castle, their beloved,
crumbling home, is going to be sold.
Then they meet their long-lost ghostly
ancestors, and everything changes
overnight! Soon, it's all hands to the
pump to save Quagmire Castle –
with hilarious results no one could
ever have imagined!

First published 2003 by
A & C Black Publishers Ltd
37 Soho Square, London, W1D 3QZ

www.acblack.com

ISBN 0-7136-6572-6

A CIP catalogue for this book is available from the British Library.

A&C Black uses paper produced with elemental chlorine-free
pulp, harvested from managed sustained forests.

Printed and bound in Spain by G. Z. Printek, Bilbao.

KAREN WALLACE

QUIRKY TIMES AT QUAGMIRE CASTLE

Illustrated by Helen Flook

A & C Black • London

To the incredible Carrie

CHAPTER ONE

Gordon Grabbit wrinkled his nose as if there was a bad smell in the air and stared at Quagmire Castle. He didn't see wonderful turrets that needed a bit of patching here and there or a few stone windows whose leaded panes were broken. He didn't notice that the front door was made out of carved oak with metal fastenings that were over four hundred years old. All Gordon Grabbit saw was a falling-down ruin that could do with a good bulldozing and a few direct hits with a wrecking ball. And Gordon Grabbit knew he was right. Because Gordon Grabbit was a bank manager and bank managers are always right. Especially where lending money is concerned.

Too much money had already been lent to Tabitha Nightshade to look after Quagmire Castle and that was a state of affairs Gordon Grabbit didn't approve of at all. Particularly because he hated anything old that took up space. You could fit fifty bungalows, each with a tiny garden and room for a two-car garage, if you knocked down the castle, filled in the lake and pulled out the maze and gardens. Gordon Grabbit's palms began to sweat just thinking about it. He took a deep breath and walked up the gravel drive towards the huge carved-oak door.

* * *

Aunt Tabitha Nightshade climbed up the specially-made stepladder and eased herself on to the seat in front of her giant sewing machine. She bent her silver-haired head forwards as she pulled the purple thread from a huge spool in and out of the various loops and eyes and finally through the giant needle, and out the other side.

Aunt Tabitha could only think straight when she was sewing so she had built an enormous machine that she could sit at for hours, sewing miles and miles of material together. Recently, she had so much thinking to do that every day echoed with the pounding of her sewing machine. And when Aunt Tabitha sewed all day, everyone at Quagmire Castle knew there was trouble afoot. She was just about to line up an extra-long piece of cloth when the front door knocker banged hard, twice.

With a sigh, Aunt Tabitha climbed back down the stepladder, shut the door of her sewing room and walked into the front hall.

* * *

'Face it,' said Gordon Grabbit, ten minutes later. 'You've got no choice.' He stuffed a piece of shortbread into his mouth and slurped a cup of tea at the same time. 'You've got to sell.'

Aunt Tabitha put her delicate porcelain teacup back on its saucer. 'But, Mr Grabbit,' she protested, 'you don't understand, Quagmire Castle has been in my family for five hundred years.'

Gordon Grabbit wiped some crumbs off his trousers on to the floor. 'Times change,' he said nastily. 'Some people get left behind.'

He bit into another biscuit. 'Anyway, bungalows are very attractive,' he blurted, spraying more crumbs on the floor.

Aunt Tabitha stared at the fat-faced bank manager whose eating habits were truly disgusting. 'Are you suggesting I move to a bungalow?'

'Of course not,' said Gordon Grabbit, quickly. He had not expected the old lady to be so difficult. He opened his briefcase and put a piece of thick white paper on the table between them. SALE OF QUAGMIRE CASTLE was written on the top. 'Unless you raise the money to pay back your loan by next week, the bank will sell Quagmire Castle and that's final.'

Aunt Tabitha looked down at the paper.

'Would you like a pen?' asked Gordon Grabbit eagerly.

'Certainly not,' replied Aunt Tabitha. She stood up and opened the door of her sitting room. 'If you will excuse me, I have some sewing to do.'

Gordon Grabbit fought back the irritation that prickled his greasy brush-cut hair. He decided to try the 'softly-softly' approach. 'I do understand how difficult it must be for you.'

'Do you indeed?' said Aunt Tabitha crisply. 'Then in that case, you can save me some time and show yourself out.'

Gordon Grabbit stood up and narrowed his pale piggy eyes. 'I'll leave you my pen. You're going to need it.' Then he turned on his heel and strode out of the room.

Five minutes later, the sound of the great sewing machine hammered through the house. But try as she might, Aunt Tabitha couldn't think of any way she could save Quagmire Castle and the more she sewed the more unhappy she became.

* * *

'Something's on Aunt Tabitha's mind,' said Jack as he and his sister, Emily, sat in a rowing boat on Toadspawn Lake. It was a still summer day and the sound of the sewing machine clattered over the air. 'She's been sewing for two days now.'

Emily looked down at a water lily. An enormous green frog was watching her with unblinking golden eyes. The extraordinary thing was that no matter how closely she stared at it, the frog showed no sign of being frightened. Indeed, it was almost as if it was listening to what Jack was saying.

'Do you think we should ask?' said Emily. 'Last time this happened, it turned out she was sewing a cover for the roof.' She grinned. 'Maybe she's found a way to sew new windows for the tower.'

Jack dipped the oars in the soupy green water and shook his head. 'I think it's more than that. Yesterday I went down to the kitchen and Mrs Gristle said Aunt Tabitha is only eating sardine paste sandwiches.'

'Ugh!' Emily pulled a face. 'What on earth for?'

'She said it was good for her brain and she needed all the help she could get.' Jack shook his head. 'There's something wrong, I'm sure there is.'

There was a loud *plop*! Emily looked down. The enormous green frog had disappeared.

* * *

Up in the West Tower, where nobody had been for almost five hundred years, Delicia Nightshade stared at her silvery fingers and tried to remember the days when she could see her reflection in the mirror.

It was a long time ago, too long to count, really. And Delicia wasn't terribly keen on remembering her age. Anyway, judging from her beautiful hands and her finely-turned ankles, she was sure she was still as beautiful as she had been in those far-off days when she travelled by coach and her servants were dressed in velvet breeches and silk waistcoats in the Nightshade colours of black and red.

Not that Delicia wanted to go back in time. She liked living in the West Tower of Quagmire Castle. Nobody knew they were there so nobody bothered them. Besides, she had Dudley for company and somehow, time seemed to fly if you could fly yourself. Delicia sighed and floated over to the window. Thinking about flying reminded her that Dudley hadn't yet returned from one of his little excursions.

After alchemy, he had taken up spellcraft and taught himself to change into anything he wanted. Right now, he was obsessed with frogs. And since it had been his idea originally to dig a lake for the castle, he had decided to take a closer look at how the water lilies were getting on and whether the bright yellow kingcups were still growing in the far corner. Also, it had to be admitted that from time to time Dudley reminded Delicia of a frog. He had an irritating habit of jumping up behind her when she was doing her tapestry. There had been many occasions when she would have stabbed her finger with her needle if her fingers hadn't been transparent ...

At that moment, Dudley suddenly appeared by her side. Water dripped from his glossy black hair and a piece of pondweed hung from his ear. Delicia pulled a face. This was the second time he had flown off in his best clothes.

'They'll shrink, you know,' she said, trying not to sound cross.

'No, they won't,' cried Dudley, peering out the window. 'They'll grow. They're only little because we see them from up here.'

Delicia stared at her husband as if he were mad. 'Have you been drinking that green stuff again?' she asked suspiciously.

'Certainly not,' replied Dudley. 'Anyway, how was I to know it wasn't peppermint cordial?' It was an episode neither of them wanted to remember. Dudley had changed himself into a bee and had nearly drowned in a glass of green stuff at some outdoor festivity. 'Where the bee sipped, there sipped I,' he added sulkily.

'Humph,' said Delicia. 'And remember where it got us.' It was only by sheer good fortune that Delicia had turned herself into a blackbird that day and had been able to rescue him.

'Let's not talk about it,' muttered Dudley, his lower lip sticking out like a church doorstep.

'As you wish, my darling,' cried Delicia gaily. That was one of the great things about being a ghost. Bad moods never lasted more than a split second. 'Perhaps I misunderstood you.'

Dudley's face lit up with a smile. 'That's the answer, my sweet,' he said, kissing her lightly on her silver cheek. He pointed down at Jack and Emily who were crossing the lawn. 'I was talking of the little ones who live in the house.' He flicked the pondweed off his ear. 'You see, I was sitting on a water lily, listening—'

At that moment, a monkey with glossy grey fur jumped down from the chandelier, spun three times in the air and landed upside-down on the floor.

Dudley and Delicia stared, wide-eyed and trembling at each other. They were both thinking the same thing. When Powderball spun three times and landed upside down it was a sure sign that something was wrong.

And it was something to do with Quagmire Castle.

CHAPTER TWO

Jack and Emily stood in the middle of Aunt Tabitha's sitting room and stared in dismay at the plates of curling sardine paste sandwiches that lay stacked up on the tables. It was clear to both of them that if Aunt Tabitha had been hoping to improve her brainpower, it hadn't worked.

Aunt Tabitha looked up from her desk. 'Sit down, dears,' she said in a tired voice. 'I'm afraid I have some rather bad news to tell you.'

Jack and Emily looked at each other and quickly sat down on the sofa.

'Gordon Grabbit, the bank manager, came to see me,' said Aunt Tabitha slowly. 'He is refusing to lend me any more money to look after Quagmire Castle. He wants me to sell.'

'Oh, no!' cried Jack.

Emily went white as a sheet and fought back the tears that welled up in her eyes.

'I've tried and tried to think of a way to solve the problem,' said Aunt Tabitha, pointing out the plates of sandwiches. 'But I haven't come up with any answers so far. And we're beginning to run out of time.'

She picked up a huge pile of papers. 'You see, after paying the bank the money I owe them for giving me loans in the first place, I haven't any money left to pay the bills.'

'I don't understand,' cried Jack. 'Why is Mr Grabbit being so mean?'

'Bank managers don't think like we do,' sighed Aunt Tabitha. 'I'm sure when he looks at Quagmire Castle all he sees is a ruin that should be pulled down.'

'It needs looking after, not pulling down!' Emily buried her face in her hands.

'What are you going to do, Aunt Tabitha?' asked Jack miserably.

'I'm going to sew a cover for Toadspawn Lake,' replied Aunt Tabitha firmly. 'The old one is full of holes and as you know, sometimes I have my best ideas when I sew. At any rate, it's my last chance and I'm never eating another sardine paste sandwich in my life.'

Emily looked up. 'Can we help?'

'We'll do anything!' cried Jack.

Aunt Tabitha forced herself to smile. 'Perhaps if we all think as hard as we can, someone will come up with the right idea.'

At that moment, Herbert Flubber, the gardener, drove by on his precious bright red and black ride-on lawn mower. He was wearing what looked like a yellow lampshade with aerials sticking out of it on his head.

'I've made Herbert a thinking cap,' said Aunt Tabitha proudly. 'Mrs Gristle has one, too. But hers is purple.' She looked at Jack and Emily, 'I don't suppose—'

'No thank you, Aunt Tabitha,' said Emily quickly. 'Besides, you'll be far too busy sewing the cover for Toadspawn Lake.'

'Of course I will,' cried Aunt Tabitha. Then she shook her head as if she had suddenly remembered something. 'There is one other problem.'

Jack and Emily stared at her. 'What?'

'We haven't got much time,' said Aunt Tabitha. 'Gordon Grabbit's coming back next week.'

* * *

Jack and Emily slowly climbed the curling wooden stairs to the second floor. 'How about a bring and buy sale?' said Emily. 'We could raise lots of money like that.'

'Not enough to pay off that horrible bank manager,' muttered Jack. 'Someone would have to donate a sack of gold or a suitcase of ten-pound notes.'

'How about a raffle?'

'What could we raffle?' asked Jack. 'We'd

need an emerald the size of a pigeon's egg.'

'Then *you* come up with some ideas!' cried Emily.

'Sorry,' said Jack. 'I didn't mean to criticise.' He shook his head. 'I just can't bear the idea of Aunt Tabitha having to sell Quagmire Castle.'

By now they had reached the top of the stairs on the third floor. Suddenly Jack froze and pointed to the end of the wood-panelled corridor. 'What's that?'

A long-haired monkey was sitting on the carpet.

It had glossy fur the colour of pewter, and orange eyes. As soon as it saw Jack and Emily, it leapt into the air, bounced off the walls and landed on its hands. Then it stared at them and did handsprings down the corridor.

'Jack,' whispered Emily, 'I think this, uh, monkey wants us to follow him.'

Jack looked puzzled. 'But there's nowhere to go. The corridor's a dead end.'

Ahead of them the monkey cartwheeled slowly forwards.

'Let's follow him anyway,' whispered Emily.

At that moment, a door they had never seen before appeared in the wall in front of them. It was a heavy, old-fashioned door with a big iron lock. Jack was just about to put his hand out to see if it was real when the monkey walked straight through it and so, to their utter astonishment, did Jack and Emily!

The next second they were standing at the bottom of a spiral stone staircase. The extraordinary thing, Emily realised later, was that neither of them felt in the least bit frightened. The monkey scampered up the steps and they went up after him.

At last when they were both almost dizzy with climbing, another door appeared in front of them. This one was decorated with metal fastenings that were strangely familiar.

'They're the same as the front door of the castle,' whispered Jack. As he spoke, the monkey rapped out a signal. Two short knocks with a pause followed by two more and a second later the door swung open.

Even though they both knew it was rude to stare, Jack and Emily stared until they thought their eyes would boggle. In front of them stood a man and a woman. The woman was dressed in a black velvet gown embroidered with gold thread. Her hair hung down to her shoulders like the mane of a white pony and her eyes were blue as sapphires. Beside her stood a man with long, curly hair, wearing a black and red chequered doublet with puffed sleeves. A gleaming sword hung from a leather belt around his waist. His eyes shone like coals in his broad pale face.

Jack stopped staring and forced himself to think. He had seen these two people before – but where? Could they have been a dream or in a history book? Suddenly, he remembered and yet the answer seemed incredible.

'Are you the um, people in the portraits downstairs?' he stammered.

'Greetings fair mortals, pray pass through our portals!' cried the curly-haired man. As he stepped forward, his sword clanked and he squared his shoulders just like in the portrait in the front hall. 'Lord Dudley Nightshade at your service and this is my dear wife, the Lady Delicia.'

'Right on! Way to go!' Delicia Nightshade beckoned Jack and Emily inside and grinned happily. She'd read the magazines that had occasionally been chucked over the garden walls and she wanted to use modern words to make these young things as comfortable as possible.

Emily looked at her feet. The strange monkey was nowhere to be seen.

'Don't worry about Powderball,' said Delicia. 'He's got, like, his own agenda.' She put her silvery hand on Emily's shoulder and steered her into the room. 'Now, let's talk. We don't have a lot of time.'

Emily stared at Delicia's extraordinary blue eyes. 'Can you read minds?'

'Of course! We can do just about anything we like.' Delicia grinned. 'I mean, you've gotta have something going for you if you're gonna be a ghost.'

Dudley led the way across a dark polished floor to a group of chairs and pushed a table covered in cards to one side.

'We started that game in 1597,' announced Delicia. She laughed. 'Snap's my favourite.'

'Excuse me,' said Emily slowly. 'But are you saying you've lived here since 1597?'

'Quagmire Castle is our home,' said Delicia simply. Suddenly her silvery face went serious. 'And we want it to stay that way. That's why we sent Powderball to fetch you.'

Jack stared in amazement. 'How do you know

about Gordon Grabbit and Aunt Tabitha?'

'First, I turned myself into a frog and listened to you talking on the lake,' said Dudley, proudly. 'Then I turned myself into a spider and crouched under her desk.'

'And I was a fly and sat on the window ledge,' said Delicia. She grinned. 'Actually it's quite fun being a fly. You get to make that buzzing noise by waggling your wings really fast.'

'Delicia!' said Dudley sternly. 'We are not here to talk about you being a fly. We are here to find a way to save Quagmire Castle.'

Emily found herself looking between Jack and Dudley and noticing for the first time that they both had the same broad face and piercing eyes. It was the strangest feeling in the world to find out that you looked like a ghost.

Jack leaned forward on his leather-backed chair. 'If you heard everything then you know that Aunt Tabitha has to come up with some money by next week or that horrible Gordon Grabbit will force her to sell.'

'I've taken care of that,' replied Delicia proudly. 'There's a sack of gold at the end of a rope tied to your rowing boat. She can pay him off with that for the time being.' She paused, remembering her magazines. 'It's the bigger picture we're looking at here.'

'I don't see any big pictures,' said Dudley in a

puzzled voice.

Delicia rolled her eyes and Emily cleared her throat. 'I think Lady Delicia is saying we all want a permanent solution to the problem.'

'Then why didn't she say so?' asked Lord Dudley.

'Would you care for some mead?' murmured Delicia smoothly. 'It's an old recipe of my grandmother's. She was given it at a staging post on her way to her estates in Scotland.'

'What's mead?' asked Emily.

'What's a staging post?' asked Jack.

Delicia and Dudley exchanged looks. They didn't have to speak to know what each other was thinking. Don't they learn anything in schools these days?

'Mead is a wine made from honey,' said Delicia.

'And a staging post is where you stop to partake of refreshment and change horses,' explained Dudley.

'You mean a bit like a hotel?' asked Jack.

'Exactly!' cried Delicia, who had suddenly remembered something else she had read in a magazine. 'Just like a country house hotel.'

There was a dull *thud* as Powderball fell off his stool in dead faint.

It was a sure sign something important had happened.

The room fell completely silent. Motes and beams danced in the golden afternoon sunshine. The faint smell of lavender and wax polish hung in the air. Jack and Emily and Delicia and Dudley looked at each other and they all knew they were thinking the same thing.

QUAGMIRE CASTLE COUNTRY HOUSE HOTEL!

It was a stroke of genius!

It was an inspiration!

And as far as Delicia and Dudley were concerned, it was a lot more fun than playing cards in the attic. Because even though Jack and Emily didn't know it yet, Delicia and Dudley had made a decision.

Their time had come at last!

CHAPTER THREE

Delicia spread her fine silver fingers and tried to stop her feet from tapping on the floor. Making plans was one of her favourite things to do and over five hundred years she'd had a lot of practice.

'Of course, we can turn our hand to anything,' she said, 'and naturally, we'd love to make friends and influence people.'

'And save Quagmire Castle,' added Dudley. He could see Jack and Emily were getting confused. 'That's the most important thing of all.'

Jack looked at the two extraordinary people in front of him and drew his eyebrows together. 'Uh, I don't want to seem ungrateful,' he said, 'but nowadays things have changed so much.' He paused. 'You see, most people are frightened of ghosts. I mean, you *are* ghosts, aren't you?'

'Spectres! Phantoms! Spirits! Ghosts! Call us what you like,' cried Delicia happily. 'Yes indeed, we are separate from the material world.'

'But as I said, we can change into anything,' explained Dudley. 'Why, the other day I turned into a panther.' He laughed. 'It was such fun. At first people thought I was a huge black cat.'

'You mean that was you!' Emily laughed out loud. 'It was all over the papers.'

Delicia smiled proudly at her husband. 'And it's not just animals. We do humans, too.' She turned to Jack and Emily. 'So you see, we could be really useful and if something gets tricky, all we do is—'

Delicia and Dudley disappeared.

Jack and Emily looked at each other. It was all so weird that neither of them could think of anything to say, so they looked round the room. At one end there was a long oak table covered in a tapestry and two silver candlesticks. Woven rugs lay on the dark wooden floor and a wooden chest with a carved brass lock sat under the window. It was a small room with beams set in the walls, and bunches of dried lavender hung from the huge timbers that held up the ceiling. There was nothing spooky or strange about it all. It just felt very, very old.

'First things first,' said Jack at last. 'Let's see if there really is a sack of gold tied to the end of a rope on Toadspawn Lake!'

* * *

'Goodness me!' Aunt Tabitha pressed her hand to the front of her lacy blouse. 'This is all too fantastical! I do believe I shall have to sit down!'

On the floor in the middle of the room was a slimy wet sack full of Elizabethan coins. As Jack had said – and it was only a little white lie – it must have been there for hundreds of years, and it was sheer luck that their fishing hook had caught on the ragged canvas.

'We've counted it out, Aunt Tabitha,' said Emily, quickly. 'There's enough to stop Mr Grabbit from forcing you to sell and some left over.'

'I must say, I am rather intrigued by this idea of turning Quagmire Castle into a country house hotel,' murmured Aunt Tabitha. 'I do know something about them myself, you know.' She picked up her embroidery needle and began stabbing tiny stitches into the corner of the cover for Toadspawn Lake. After sewing, she did her best thinking when she was embroidering. In no time at all, she had made a butterfly crouched on a leaf.

'Have you ever stayed in one?' asked Jack.

'Certainly not,' replied Aunt Tabitha. 'They're far too expensive!' She threaded her needle with blue silk and began to make a dragonfly. 'I read all about them the last time I went to the dentist. I remember it very well. All you need is a lovely home with a beautiful garden and delicious food. Then your guests pay you lots and lots of money.' She beamed. 'What clever children you are!'

'It was Delicia's idea,' blurted Emily. Jack kicked her under the table and she went bright red.

'I beg your pardon, dear.'

'Delicious food is a brilliant idea,' said Jack.

'Thank you, dear.' Aunt Tabitha pulled out a tiny pair of scissors and clipped the last knot on the dragonfly. 'I can't wait to see Mr Grabbit's face when I tell him.' She paused. 'There is one thing ...'

Jack and Emily held their breath.

'We'll have rather a lot to do and not much time to do it in.'

'Don't worry, Aunt Tabitha,' said Jack, firmly. He winked at Emily. 'We'll see it through.'

At that moment, there was a knock on the door and Mrs Gristle appeared in the room. Mrs Gristle had the reddest face and the meatiest arms you could imagine. In fact, Emily often thought that Mrs Gristle looked like a huge ham hock in an apron.

'Mr Grabbit to see you, ma'am.' Mrs Gristle scowled. 'Shall I tell him you're busy?'

'Goodness me, no!' cried Aunt Tabitha, standing up and shaking a shower of rainbow threads from her skirt. 'Show him in immediately. I have something very important to tell him.'

* * *

Fifteen minutes later, Gordon Grabbit stood whacking the legs of his shiny trousers with a sheaf of papers. He had a face like thunder. 'You'll regret this,' he snarled. He glared at the lumpy wet sack on the carpet. 'Your pile of coins is all very well but it's not going to last long enough to save Quagmire Castle.'

'Old gold is just as good as new gold, Mr. Grabbit,' said Aunt Tabitha. 'And it will last long enough to serve our purposes.'

'That'll be the day,' said Gordon Grabbit. 'You've never been able to keep up with your payments.' He banged the papers down on the table. 'I'll be back again next week.'

'That won't be necessary,' said Aunt Tabitha in a dignified voice.

'Oh, yes it will,' snapped Gordon Grabbit.

'Oh, no it won't,' replied Aunt Tabitha and she picked up the papers and threw them into the fire. 'You see, Mr Grabbit. By the end of next week, I shall never need your bank's services again.'

'Huh!' muttered Gordon Grabbit, rudely. 'Pigs have wings.'

At that moment, Jack and Emily saw a large pink pig with an enormous grin on its face fly past the window. And even though it had a curly tail and a snout and a pair of bristly ears, there was no disguising the black glittering eyes of Dudley Nightshade!

At the same moment, Herbert Flubber looked up from raking the front drive. He was still wearing the thinking cap Aunt Tabitha had given him but now his face was a white as a candle. There was a clatter of gravel as he crumpled to the ground.

'Oh dear, poor Herbert!' cried Aunt Tabitha. 'He's been thinking too hard. I must tell him our wonderful news!'

'What news?' asked Gordon Grabbit suspiciously.

Aunt Tabitha held out her hand as if she hadn't heard him. 'Goodbye, Mr Grabbit. I hope you won't mind if you show yourself out.'

'I don't know what you're scheming,' said Gordon Grabbit, glaring at Jack and Emily. 'But you won't get away with it.'

Jack and Emily didn't reply. They knew if they opened their mouths they would burst out laughing.

As Gordon Grabbit loaded the coins into his briefcase and Aunt Tabitha bent over Herbert Flubber on the drive, the pig with the coal black eyes flew past the window again.

But this time he was upside down!

* * *

That evening, Aunt Tabitha asked everyone to a special business supper in the dining room. After they had finished eating, she thanked Mrs Gristle for her delicious food and Herbert Flubber for his fabulous flower arrangements. And she thanked Jack and Emily for coming up with the brilliant idea in the first place. Then she pulled on a rope and a huge purple satin banner dropped down from the ceiling. QUAGMIRE CASTLE – OPEN FOR BUSINESS was sewn in huge gold letters across the front.

'So you see,' said Aunt Tabitha, beaming. 'I've

been busy, too.'

Jack and Emily stood up with clipboards in their hands. They had also been busy. If Quagmire Castle was to become a country house hotel, there was a lot of work to do. All the bedrooms had to be cleaned and redecorated. The kitchen had to be made bigger so that Mrs Gristle would be able to cope with preparing the extra food. And of course the garden would have to be mown every day as well as flowers picked for the rooms, and the maze clipped and kept tidy.

As Emily and then Jack read out their lists, everyone's faces grew longer and longer. How on earth would they do it all in time? And they all knew what would happen if they didn't.

Suddenly, there was a knock on the door and two extraordinary-looking people walked into the room.

The man was dressed in an old-fashioned evening suit and carried a ladder and a bucket. And the woman was wearing a leopard-spotted leotard with a scarlet cloak thrown around her shoulders. In one hand she held a huge feather duster and in the other hand a painter's palette.

Jack and Emily exchanged a secret grin. Lord Dudley and Lady Delicia Nightshade had come down from the attic!

'Good evening, dear lady!' cried Dudley,

fixing Aunt Tabitha with his coal-black eyes. 'I must apologise for the lateness of the hour but we understand you are in need of assistance.' He turned and smiled at Mrs Gristle and Herbert Flubber. Beside him, Delicia's own eyes sparkled like sapphires.

It must have been something in their eyes, thought Emily, later. It didn't occur to Aunt Tabitha or anyone else for that matter to question how two complete strangers could turn up in the night and offer to help turn Quagmire Castle into a country house hotel.

Aunt Tabitha stood up. 'Why, yes—'

'Dudley,' cried Dudley, bowing.

'Delicia,' said Delicia with a smile.

Aunt Tabitha smiled in return. Even Mrs Gristle and Herbert Flubber's long faces disappeared. 'Why, yes, Dudley and Delicia. We do need some help. How very kind.'

She turned and introduced everyone around the table. 'This is my nephew, Jack, and niece, Emily. Mrs Gristle, the cook, and Herbert Flubber, the gardener.'

'Charmed,' cried Delicia.

'Delighted,' said Dudley.

They sat down beside Jack and Emily and gave them such big winks and grins, both of them were sure Aunt Tabitha would spot something suspicious. But Aunt Tabitha didn't notice a thing.

'How lovely,' said Aunt Tabitha, sitting down herself. 'Now, tell me, what can you do best?'

'We can do everything, dear lady,' said Dudley smoothly. He touched the lapel of his old-fashioned evening suit. 'I can run your restaurant.' He pointed to his ladder. 'I can repaint your castle.'

'And I can clean and decorate every room you require,' said Delicia.

'That sounds absolutely wonderful,' cried Aunt Tabitha. 'How long would it take?'

Delicia and Dudley looked puzzled as if they were trying hard to give the right answer.

'Six minutes,' said Delicia.

'Six minutes?' gasped Aunt Tabitha.

'Six hours,' corrected Dudley.

'Six hours?' spluttered Mrs Gristle.

'Six days,' said Jack quickly. He stared into Delicia's glittering blue eyes. 'That's what you mean, isn't it?'

'Of course it is!' shrieked Delicia. 'Silly me! Six days!' She threw back her head and hooted with laughter. 'And you'll never even know we're here!'

CHAPTER FOUR

Emily stared at the two oval portraits of Lord Dudley and Lady Delicia Nightshade that hung in the front hall. 'It's all very well those um—'

'Ghosts,' suggested Jack calmly.

'Well, I know they are ghosts in some ways,' said Emily. 'In most ways, I guess.' She shook her head. 'The thing is, I'm pretty sure they'd have some crazy ideas and it would be almost impossible to stop them.'

At that moment, three paint rollers and a large tray of yellow paint sailed past their heads and took off up the stairs. They were followed by two Hoovers, three dustpans and brushes and a long procession of feather dusters. The moment they had disappeared, Aunt Tabitha opened her sitting room door.

'You'll never believe what's happened, dears,' she cried. Her face was pink with excitement. 'I put an advertisement in the papers two days ago and we're fully booked already!' She looked around at the newly-painted hall and the huge Turkish carpet that had appeared overnight. 'So

I've made a big decision.'

A funny feeling prickled at the back of Emily's neck. When Aunt Tabitha made a 'big' decision, something peculiar always happened.

'We're making such good progress, I've decided to open on Saturday!'

'What?' cried Jack and Emily together. 'But—'

'No buts,' replied Aunt Tabitha in a happy, tinkling voice. 'I've spoken to Dudley and Delicia and they think it's a perfectly splendid idea.'

'But what about the kitchen?' asked Emily. 'It's still far too small.'

'Dudley made it bigger last night,' said Aunt Tabitha. 'Of course, at first Mrs Gristle wasn't sure about cooking over an open fire and she'd never used a spit before. But she soon got the hang of it.' Aunt Tabitha laughed. 'She's says it's almost faster than a microwave once Dudley's got the fire roaring.'

'A spit?' croaked Jack.

'An open fire?' gasped Emily.

Aunt Tabitha clapped her hands delightedly. 'Isn't it so wonderfully old-fashioned? Just like a real castle!'

Emily put her hands over her face. 'But what about fire extinguishers?'

'Dudley's thought of that,' said Aunt Tabitha firmly. 'There's a bucket of water by the door.'

She turned. 'By the way, have you seen the dining room? Delicia finished it last night.'

A moment later, Jack and Emily stood in the dining room and stared. The floor was strewn with rushes and rose petals. On one wall were the heads of bristly wild boar with great curved tusks and deer with enormous antlers. Crossed spears and painted armour decorated either end. On the other wall, huge carrots were arranged in patterns around swedes and parsnips and the whole thing was splattered with hundreds of sticky green peas.

'Delicia's so clever,' trilled Aunt Tabitha. 'Even vegetarians will love eating here.'

Before Jack and Emily could reply, the telephone began to ring and Aunt Tabitha hurried from the room.

'I think we'd better have a look upstairs,' said Jack.

Emily nodded. 'Do you think they've put everyone under a spell?'

'Everyone but us,' replied Jack, rolling his eyes.

* * *

'I told you to wait!' cried Delicia crossly. She turned. 'And I told you to stay where you were!'

Emily couldn't believe her eyes. On one side of the huge bedroom, two Hoovers stood hanging their heads as if they had done something they weren't supposed to do. Floating below the ceiling, a four-poster bed and three chairs seemed to be trying to keep as still as possible. Half the walls were painted bright turquoise with shocking pink zigzags running most of the way around the room.

Delicia looked at the expression on Emily's face. 'Don't worry,' she said gaily. 'They lost concentration. They'll be fine in a minute.'

Something moved impatiently in the corner of the room. It was the pink paint brush and it was obviously fed up with waiting.

'No,' said Delicia firmly, as if she were talking to a dog. 'Not until I tell you.'

She sighed good-naturedly and led Emily from the room. 'Come with me and let me show you what I've done in the bathrooms!'

* * *

Dudley knew about mazes. After all, he had designed the one at Quagmire Castle. And now the hedges were so high and beautifully trimmed by the lovely Herbert Flubber that you could get properly lost if you took the wrong turning. Dudley chuckled to himself. Every turning was the wrong turning.

What Dudley didn't know much about was designing flowerbeds. On the whole he'd left that sort of thing up to Delicia. Now here he was on his own, trying to remember whether hearts or diamonds or clubs were the best shapes for gardens.

In the end, he had gone for his favourite shape. It was the easiest thing to do and now he thought it looked fantastic. He turned himself into a vulture and sat on the roof to admire his handiwork.

Four beds in the shape of a skull and cross bones were beautifully planted in his favourite colours. Red and black stripes with white for the skull part, of course.

Dudley flapped lazily over the lawn Herbert

was mowing.

Poor Herbert! He took one look at the vulture circling above him and drove straight into Toadspawn Lake!

* * *

'Don't be ridiculous,' snapped Gordon Grabbit. 'That's not a vulture. It's a pigeon.'

'If I say it's a vulture, it's a vulture,' said his older sister, Cynthia. She turned to her husband who sat in the back, carving his initials into the rented car's leather seat. 'Isn't that right, Eddy?'

'Of course it is,' said Eddy, turning his attention to the carpet. 'But we're not here to go bird-watching. We're here to talk about our investment.' He yanked open the car door and pointed to the huge purple banner with the huge golden letters. 'And you never told us nothing about this, did ya?'

Gordon Grabbit went bright red. All his life he'd wanted to impress his older sister. Ever since she had got into the property business and become a millionaire virtually overnight, Gordon was desperate to get into her good books so he could be one, too. Quagmire Castle was supposed to be his big chance.

'It's perfect,' he had told his sister. 'Crumbling old castle, lots of land. Fill in the lake and bingo! Fifty bungalows with their own backyards!'

Cynthia Swipe had narrowed her pale piggy

44

eyes. 'What about the owner?'

'Easy peasy. The old lady owes the bank a fortune.' Gordon Grabbit had looked smug. 'All I gotta do is call in the loan. We'll make a fortune!'

Now he stared at the purple banner with the huge gold letters – QUAGMIRE CASTLE – OPEN FOR BUSINESS – and a sweaty rage surged through his body. He'd been cheating Tabitha Nightshade out of money to make her broke for as long as he could remember. How dare she ruin his plans now?

Eddy Swipe picked at a gold tooth with the point of his knife. 'So what are we going to do, big boy?' he asked in a mean voice. 'We can't exactly break the old lady's arm, can we?'

'Ah, shuddup, Eddy,' said Cynthia. 'I'll think of something.'

'Like what?'

Cynthia shot her husband a poisonous look. 'Like, I booked us into the best room on the first night.' She shrugged. 'Who knows, maybe the place will get flooded 'cos someone leaves the bath running.'

Eddy Swipe's three gold teeth sparkled in the sun.

Cynthia's fat face gleamed with her own incredible cleverness. 'There's only one way to make money and that's the dirty way.' She turned to where her brother was staring at her with adoration in his eyes. 'Got it, Gordon?'

'Got it, sis.'

Above them the vulture cocked his head. His coal black eyes flashed with anger. No one noticed as he circled above them and flew back towards Quagmire Castle.

CHAPTER FIVE

Damian Sponge gripped the wheel of his Jaguar sports car with black-gloved hands. Beside him, Velveteen Gray admired the long fake nails she had fixed to the ends of her stubby fingers. She particularly liked the dull purple polish she had chosen. Damian's eyes flicked sideways at her outstretched hands.

'Why'd you choose the same colour as your nose?' he asked as he swung the car sideways so it lurched round what was barely a bend in the road.

'There's no need to be rude,' said Velveteen Gray in a tight voice. 'Purple is in. Everyone is wearing it.' She looked at his spotted cravat and the yellow v-neck pullover that stretched over his bulging stomach. 'Besides, one of us has to look the part.' Before he could think of anything rude to say in reply, she pulled out a leather bound folder from her briefcase. 'Sponge and Gray, Hotel Inspectors with the Highest Standards' was stamped in red letters on the front.

'So what do you know about Quagmire Castle?' asked Velveteen Gray. 'Apart from the fact we're staying there tonight.'

'It's new so it will be nervous.' Damian slammed his foot down on the accelerator and the car shot down the middle of the country lane.

* * *

'So what if it *was* a castle,' squealed Norman Breadsop. He ran his greasy fingers through his carrot-coloured hair and down the front of his KIDS FIRST t-shirt. 'Castles are stupid. I want a hotel with a fruit machine and a swimming pool.'

Beside him, his sister, Trixie, had a face like a ferret and ragged black hair that was full of knots. She looked up from the horror comic she was reading. 'Do you mean it hasn't got a swimming pool?' she shrieked at the top of her voice. 'I'm not staying in a hotel with no swimming pool.'

In the front seat, their father, Simon, felt his own hair turn greyer and go thinner. His wife, Sybil, trembled in the passenger seat and he could see her knuckles had turned white. 'It has a lovely lake, Trixie darling. And a maze.'

'Great,' muttered Norman. 'You can both get lost!'

'I beg your pardon, dear?' murmured Sybil Breadsop.

'Nothing.' Norman stared furiously out of the window and blew an enormous bubble of gum, which stuck to the glass.

'I don't see why we have to go away in the first place,' whined Trixie. 'All my friends are shopping this weekend.'

'Big deal,' hissed Norman. 'Mine are shoplifting.'

'We're going away because your father and I need a little break,' said Mrs Breadsop in a small, weary voice. 'And it's nice to be all together.'

Norman and Trixie rolled their eyes and pulled faces at each other. Contempt for their parents was the only thing they had in common.

* * *

Emily was carrying a huge bunch of red and white roses she had picked from Herbert Flubber's extraordinary new flowerbeds when she saw Powderball doing handsprings at the end of the corridor. 'Oh, no,' she said out loud.

'What's the matter?' asked Jack, who had just hung another huge shiny QUAGMIRE CASTLE banner from the roof. Aunt Tabitha had made it that morning and insisted it be displayed immediately.

Emily nodded in the direction of Powderball, who was bouncing up and down and looking more agitated by the minute. 'He wants us to follow him and the first guests are supposed to arrive in half an hour.'

Jack stared in the monkey's burning orange eyes. 'Come on,' he said, running down the corridor. 'If there's trouble, we'd better find out about it now.'

Emily jammed the bunch of roses into a bucket of water which had mysteriously appeared at her feet and ran after Jack as fast as she could.

Five minutes later, she sat on a wooden stool, watching as Dudley paced back and forth, waving his sword angrily. 'This Gordon Grabbit,' he shouted. 'I shall hang, draw and quarter him. Who did you say he was?'

'Aunt Tabitha's bank manager,' replied Jack.

Even though he had always thought Gordon Grabbit was rather disgusting, never once did he imagine he was an out and out cheat. If what Dudley had heard was true, then Aunt Tabitha must be warned straightaway.

'She won't believe you,' said Delicia, reading his mind. 'Besides it will only upset her on the opening night. Especially since Mrs Gristle is making a special banquet to welcome the new guests. No,' she said firmly, shaking her long silver hair. 'This is something we will have to sort ourselves.'

Emily thought of the Hoovers fighting over the carpets while the beds and chairs floated patiently below the ceiling. The idea of Delicia sorting things out in her own way was somewhat worrying, especially if there were guests in the house. 'What will we do?' she asked.

'I don't know yet,' replied Delicia with a faraway look in her eye. 'But I know one thing and that is no one is knocking down Quagmire Castle.'

There was a dull bang. Through the window, they could all see a plume of red smoke hanging over the woods.

'That's Herbert Flubber's signal,' cried Jack. 'The guests have just come through the gates. We've got to go.'

'Keep your eyes peeled,' warned Dudley.

'And don't worry, we'll be there if anything goes wrong.'

'Thanks,' said Jack. 'We couldn't have got this far without you.'

'Not so fast, pardner,' said Delicia in her best Texan drawl. She grinned wolfishly. 'We ain't finished yet.'

Two minutes later Aunt Tabitha stood white-faced in the front hall. 'Mrs Gristle has just left. She has measles.'

Emily's hands flew to her face. 'What will we do about the banquet?'

As she spoke, Delicia strolled out of the dining room, dressed in a black and purple cocktail dress. A frilly white cap with a tiny vulture brooch was fixed to her hair, which she had piled up on her head. Beside her, Dudley wore a gleaming chef's hat. A meat cleaver hung from his belt and a long silver knife glittered in his hand.

'Tea?' twittered Delicia, holding out a tray of beautifully arranged tea cups and a plate of little cakes.

'My dear Dudley and Delicia! How absolutely extraordinary!' Aunt Tabitha sat down on a chair and took a cup of tea in her hands.

'Gracious! I had no idea you could—'

'We once took refuge at a staging post,' explained Delicia gaily.

'So don't you worry about anything,' added

Dudley. 'I'm a positive *dream* in the kitchen!'

Aunt Tabitha looked into Dudley's coal-black eyes. 'Do you know, dear? I do believe you are.'

'Way to go!' cried Delicia. She turned to Dudley. 'Catcha later, chefbaby!'

Dudley shot her a puzzled look and disappeared downstairs to the kitchen.

At that moment, the front door opened and Simon and Sybil Breadsop stood in the doorway with Norman and Trixie.

'See?' muttered Norman to his sister. 'What did I tellya?' He looked at the hall. 'Dumb and boring.' He blew a bubble of gum that burst with a horrible wet *pop*.

Jack and Emily stared at each other. They had never seen such disgusting children in their lives. Even Aunt Tabitha seemed taken aback.

'Welcome to Quagmire Castle!' cried Delicia, spinning on her feet. Suddenly her tray held two cups of tea and two strawberry milkshakes. 'May I offer you some refreshment?'

Norman and Trixie elbowed their parents out of the way and made a grab for the milkshakes. But as soon as their fingers touched the glass, they jumped back as if the glasses were electrified.

'Perhaps your parents might like theirs first,' said Delicia smoothly.

Mr and Mrs Breadsop picked up the teacups with trembling hands. 'Why not visit the maze,' suggested Delicia, fixing them with her sapphire eyes. 'A little peace and quiet after your journey will do you the world of good.'

Sybil and Simon Breadsop gave Delicia a look of pure gratitude and stumbled out of the house and into the garden like a pair of shell-shocked rabbits.

'What about us?' Norman gulped his milkshake and slammed the glass down on the table. 'It's our holiday, too.'

'Yeah,' said Trixie. 'And you don't even have a swimming pool.'

'We have a wonderful lake,' said Emily politely. 'I'll show it to you if you want.'

'Who wants to look at a smelly old lake?' Trixie kicked at the tassels on the Persian carpet.

'Would a playground suit you?' asked Delicia in a suspiciously helpful-sounding voice.

'Maybe.'

'Fabulous!' said Delicia. 'Aunt Tabitha will sign you in and Jack will take your cases to your rooms.' She smiled like a cat. 'And I will show you the playground.'

'It better be good,' said Norman rudely.

'It's out of this world,' replied Delicia.

Emily was about to ask what playground when the front door opened again and Cynthia Swipe click-clacked into the hall on her high-heeled shoes. Eddy oozed in behind her. As soon as Emily saw Cynthia's pale piggy eyes, she knew immediately that these were the people Dudley had warned them about.

'Nice spot you've got here,' said Eddy. He picked up a vase on the mantelpiece and turned it upside down to see where it was made and put it back again.

Cynthia Swipe held out her hand. 'Cynthia Swipe and this is my husband, Eddy.'

Aunt Tabitha shook hands and forced a smile. There was something peculiar about these people but she wasn't sure what. It was almost as if she had met them before – or the woman, anyway.

'Mind if we tour your facilities?' asked Eddy. 'There's a maze, I believe and a lake?'

Delicia stepped forward and fixed Eddy with a piercing stare. 'Allow me to guide you.' She turned to Trixie and Norman. 'I was about to show our younger guests the custom-built outdoor activity centre.'

'She means playground,' said Trixie in a sour voice.

'Do I?' asked Delicia sweetly. She turned to where Cynthia was standing, staring at Trixie and Norman. Usually Cynthia didn't like children but there was something about these two that was strangely appealing.

Delicia watched her with bright blue eyes. 'Will you join us, Mrs Swipe?' And with a swirl of her hand, she ushered them all out of the front hall.

Jack and Emily and Aunt Tabitha stood for a moment in silence.

'Our first guests!' said Aunt Tabitha in a slightly nervous voice. She straightened the collar of her lacy blouse with trembling hands. 'By the way, I forgot to ask you. Where did you meet Dudley and Delicia?'

'Oh, they were just hanging around,' said Emily smoothly.

'Ah,' said Aunt Tabitha as if that explained everything. 'Well, jolly lucky for all of us.' And she went through the door to the kitchen.

Car tyres scrunched on the drive. Emily ran to the front door and pulled it open. 'Welcome to Quagmire Castle,' she said in her friendliest voice.

Damian Sponge took his handmade pigskin overnight bag out of the boot of his dark green sports car. Beside him, Velveteen Gray flipped her coat over her arm and lifted up her own suitcase. Neither of them noticed the white card that fluttered to the ground.

'Cocktails will be served in the garden room. The banquet will be held in the dining room,' said Jack when they had signed the register.

Velveteen Gray wrinkled her nose. 'You do have a vegetarian menu, don't you?'

'Naturally, dear lady,' cried Dudley who had appeared out of nowhere and was now dressed like a headwaiter. 'We even have vegetables on the walls so vegetarians will feel right at home.'

'Allow me to show to your rooms,' said Jack quickly.

'Certainly not!' cried Dudley. 'I shall have the honour.'

'Thank you,' twittered Velveteen Gray as she stared into Dudley's coal black eyes. It was most extraordinary! She skipped up the stairs as if she had springs in her feet.

Behind her, Damian Sponge couldn't believe his eyes. He had never seen Velveteen Gray so lively. He hadn't believed it was possible.

Emily stood on the front steps. As she let her gaze pass over the high, trimmed hedges of the maze and across the sparkling green lawns to the beautifully raked drive, her eye caught sight of a small white card lying by the back wheel of Damian Sponge's car. She ran across and picked it up. What she read made her heart hammer like a road drill. 'Sponge and Gray, Hotel Inspectors with the Highest Standards'. She stuffed the card in her pocket and ran to find Jack. Now it was absolutely vital that everything went smoothly on their first night. A bad review would mean disaster for Quagmire Castle.

CHAPTER SIX

Cynthia and Eddy Swipe watched in admiration as Norman set about hacking at the wooden climbing frame with an axe he had found in the potting shed. Earlier, Trixie had impressed them by snapping through most of the chain links on the swings with a bolt cutter so whoever used the swings next would almost certainly fall and hurt themselves.

'These youngsters could be very useful,' said Cynthia, thoughtfully. 'They've got the right attitude. I noticed it the first time I saw them.'

'Whaddyamean?' asked Eddy, who always left the planning side of things to his wife. His job was to count the money.

Cynthia turned away from the playground and sat down on a bench.

'Whaddyamean?' asked Eddy again.

'We get them to do the dirty work for us,' said Cynthia. She smiled smugly. 'They wreck the place while we're at this stupid banquet tonight.' A large sapphire-coloured dragonfly zoomed past her face and landed on the grass at her feet.

'Like I said, all it takes is a few bath taps turned in the wrong direction and a bit more fun with the axe and the bolt cutters.'

Eddy grinned and his gold teeth sparkled in the sun. 'You're a genius, my dear.'

'I know.'

Cynthia got up and headed towards the noise of splintering wood. 'Let's go and introduce ourselves.'

Five minutes later, the deal was agreed.

'Just remember,' said Eddy as he handed over a wad of notes to two pairs of dirty outstretched hands. 'The job has to be done tonight.'

Norman grinned nastily. 'We didn't have anything else planned, did we, sis?'

'Sounds like our kind of fun.' Trixie looked up from folding her money. 'Can we torch the place, too? We like bonfires.'

'Don't be dumb,' said her brother. 'We're going to flood it, don't you remember?'

'Oh yeah.'

'And bust a few things.'

Trixie nodded happily.

'So we meet after the banquet upstairs in our room,' said Eddy. He laughed. 'Or what's left of it.'

Norman and Trixie nodded and walked off into the garden. Trixie had seen some nice red and white flowers they could pull up.

'Come on,' said Cynthia. 'We'd better go and unpack. We should at least look like we're going to stay the night.'

The bright blue dragonfly soared over their heads and disappeared into an attic window.

* * *

Sybil Breadsop sat next to her husband on a patch of soft grass in the middle of the maze. In one hand she held a beautiful tulip-shaped glass of clear sparkling champagne.

'It was so clever of that lovely waiter to find

us, don't you think, dear?' She sipped at her drink. 'I do believe there is something magical about this place.'

Simon Breadsop squeezed his wife's hand. He wasn't sure whether it was the champagne or just the fact that they had been away from their children but he had not felt so happy and relaxed for as long as he could remember. 'Maybe there's something magical about being on our own,' he murmured dreamily.

A snake with shiny eyes and a black and red diamond pattern down its back slithered noiselessly under the bushes.

'Funny you should say that, dear,' said Sybil, sipping her drink once again. It was the strangest thing. It didn't matter how much she drank, the beautiful glass was always half full. 'Because I've just had the most amazing idea.'

Simon sat up. 'I've had an amazing idea, too! What's yours?'

'Mine's about the children,' said Sybil almost shyly.

Simon turned to his wife with a bright face. 'So's mine. And I don't know why I haven't thought of it before.'

Sybil grabbed her husband's hand. 'Let's send them away,' she cried. 'Far away! Far, far away!' Then she blushed and stared at her faded cotton skirt. 'I mean, far away to camp, that is.'

'For the whole summer,' said Simon gaily. He pulled his wife to her feet and hugged her. 'And for the first time ever, we won't take no for an answer.'

Sybil threw back her head and laughed. 'They'll do what they're told or else!'

'Or else!' cried Simon in a delighted voice. They held hands and danced round and around the soft grass until they were dizzy. Then they fell down and burst out laughing.

'More champagne, darling?'

'Yes, please!' Sybil watched the wonderful bubbles tumble from the neck of the bottle into her half-full glass. 'Then we must go back and change for the banquet.'

* * *

Aunt Tabitha patted the front of her pale pink lacy blouse. Her stomach felt as if it were full of a cloud of butterflies. 'I do hope the banquet will be a success,' she said to no one in particular in her sitting room. 'Everyone has worked so hard.'

'So have you, Aunt,' said Jack kindly.

'And I think you look absolutely wonderful,' said Emily. Beside her, Herbert Flubber shifted nervously in the purple evening suit with the gold braid that Aunt Tabitha had made for him the evening before. 'QC' for Quagmire Castle was embroidered on his top pocket. 'And you look lovely too, Mr Flubber,' added Emily quickly.

A tray with four tulip-shaped glasses stood in the middle of the room. Each one sparkled with champagne that Dudley had told them he'd found in the cellar. Now Aunt Tabitha handed everyone a glass.

'I think we should drink a toast, don't you?' She raised her glass. 'To Quagmire Castle Country House Hotel!'

'Quagmire Castle Country House Hotel!' cried everyone. And even though Emily and Jack had never tasted champagne before, the bubbles had trickled down their throats before they could decide whether they liked it or not.

'Don't worry about Damian Sponge and Velveteen Gray,' whispered Jack as they pretended to look out the window at a huge red sun falling into Toadspawn Lake. 'I've put them in the best rooms and Delicia said she would look after them specially.'

For the first time, Emily was beginning to feel happy and relaxed. She looked down at her brand new emerald green party dress. It had mysteriously arrived that morning, wrapped in tissue paper in a brown cardboard box. There was a parcel for Jack, too. He looked really smart in a checked jacket and bright blue trousers.

'What are smiling at?' asked Jack, watching her face.

'Us,' said Emily. 'I can't believe we're standing here and all this is happening. It's like a dream!'

'It's pretty weird, that's for sure.' Jack turned to where Aunt Tabitha was laughing and talking with Herbert Flubber. Even the gardener, who usually stood stiff as a rake, was flopped down on the sofa, looking pink and pleased with himself. Jack grinned and shook his head. 'And I don't think we're the only ones who are dreaming!'

* * *

Damian Sponge straightened his navy blazer and gave the buttons a final polish so they shone in the red-gold sunlight pouring in through the window. He had already written most of his report. The room was luxuriously, if eccentrically, furnished and even though he usually only took showers, there was something inviting about the lily pads and rose petals that floated in the bath. As for the jewel-encrusted throne that sat on a pedestal overlooking the lake, of course it was faintly ridiculous, but when he had taken the trouble to sit in it, there was something strangely appealing about it all. Not to mention the fact that it was possibly the most comfortable chair in the world.

'Humph,' muttered Damian Sponge to himself. It was a point of honour with him to find something wrong with every hotel he stayed in. 'Humph. We'll see.'

There was a faint scratching noise at his door. It sounded like a rat but it was sure to be Velveteen Gray. Damian sighed. His partner was so refined these days, she had given up knocking. 'Too definite a noise, darling,' she had explained, waving her dark purple fingernails. 'One must keep one's options open.' Of course, Damian couldn't understand what scratching at a door had to do with keeping open options, but he ignored her. Just like she ignored his crazy driving and his insistence on washing his car every time they stopped for petrol.

Damian opened the door and Velveteen skipped into the room in a pair of silver sandals with leather thongs which criss-crossed all the way up her legs. She was wearing something that looked like a cross between a bath towel and a king-sized sheet.

'My Greek look! Like it?'

'Ravishing, my dear,' replied Damian, quickly. He moved over to a table in the middle of the room where two tulip shaped-glasses sat beside a bottle of champagne in a bucket of ice. 'Drinkiepoohs?'

* * *

Cynthia Swipe squeezed her short thick body into a frilly white elasticised dress and teetered across the room in high-heeled slingbacks. She looked like a wedding cake on stilts.

In front of the mirror, Eddy brushed his black hair into a quiff, smeared it in place with gel and wiped his hands on the back of his shiny brown suit.

'Did you sort out a signal with those kids?' Cynthia drew in a pair of thin eyebrows over her piggy eyes and outlined her sharp mouth in scarlet lipstick.

Eddy nodded. 'When they bang the gong for the banquet, those kids get going with their new toys.' He grinned. 'They can't wait.'

'Nor can I.' Cynthia got up and looked around the room. 'By the way, I thought you'd ordered some drinks.'

'I did but they never arrived.'

'Useless dump. The sooner it's knocked down, the better.' She grabbed her handbag and yanked open the door. 'Come on, we'll drink to our new fortune downstairs.'

* * *

Trixie dragged her penknife across the antique leather wallpaper and pulled off a strip in her hands. 'Did you ring for room service?' She tore off another strip. 'We can't trash the joint on an empty stomach.'

Norman stood on a chair and began to pull apart the chandelier. 'It should be here any minute.'

Trixie threw herself on to the sofa and began poking holes in the stuffed arms. 'I'm starving.'

'Me too,' said Norman, from the bathroom. There was the sound of running water.

A minute later, he threw himself beside his sister and pulled her hair out of habit. She kicked him because that was what she always did. Then they began ripping up the feather cushions and hitting each other over the head.

The door flew open.

'Children! Children!' cried Dudley in his friendliest voice. He wore a long scarlet cloak and a black top hat. 'What jollity! What exuberance!'

'Who are you?' snarled Norman. 'I ordered room service, not an idiot dressed up as a magician!'

'Indeed you did,' replied Dudley gaily. 'And we'll get to that later.'

Trixie glared at him. 'If you ain't got the grub, get lost!'

'Yeah,' said Norman, yanking a curtain off its hooks. 'We got business to do.'

Dudley smiled. 'So have I, dear boy. So have I.'

'Then get on with it,' snapped Trixie. She jumped up and ripped into the wallpaper with her knife. ''Cos we're leaving this dump tonight.' She looked at him smugly. 'That's the deal.'

'What deal, dear child?' asked Dudley.

'The deal we made with Mr and Mrs Swipe,'

said Norman proudly.

Dudley threw up his hands in surprise. 'There must be some mistake. What about your dear parents? I thought they were on holiday.'

Norman stood on the sofa and stuck out his chest. 'Can't you read? KIDS RULE! We do what we want!'

'Yeah,' said Trixie, pulling off more wallpaper. 'And we don't take "no" for an answer.'

'Of course you don't,' agreed Dudley. He looked around the room. 'But after all this activity, aren't you getting a bit hungry?'

'The room service stinks,' said Norman. 'We'll steal something from the kitchen later.'

Dudley swept his scarlet cloak through the air. 'Allow me to save you the trouble.'

A gleaming silver food trolley stood in the middle of the room. It was covered in hamburgers, chips, pizzas, ice cream, and cans and cans of soft drink. It was exactly what Norman and Trixie ate every day. They rushed towards the trolley and without a word of thanks, they grabbed the food in both hands and began stuffing it into their mouths like pigs.

Which was exactly what they turned into.

You could tell which one was Trixie because her pink snout was smeared with tomato ketchup. While Norman had become huge and spotted and bristly.

'Hey!' yelled his sister. 'You look just like a pig!'

'You're a pig yourself, dumb brain,' grunted Norman.

'Don't call me a pig,' screamed Trixie. Then she saw herself in the mirror. 'Norman,' she said in a choked voice. 'Look in the mirror.'

Norman turned and found himself staring at a drooling pig wearing a KIDS RULE t-shirt. He gulped then he began to howl. 'I WANT MY MUMMY!'

'I WANT MY DADDY!' squealed Trixie and great piggy tears rolled down her face.

'Clattering cannonballs!' cried Dudley in pretend amazement. 'What on earth is this I see? A pair of pigs.' A stick appeared in his hand. 'We must remove them quickly before they do any more damage!' And without another word, he herded Norman and Trixie out in the hall and down the back stairs to a pig pen that suddenly appeared where the playground had been earlier that afternoon.

CHAPTER SEVEN

Delicia stood in the dining room and admired the extraordinary cold buffet that Dudley had created. On one end of a long sideboard lay a crispy roasted suckling pig with a pineapple in its mouth. At the other end was a huge salmon with a meat cleaver sticking out of its head. In between, laid out like a rainbow, were salads and vegetable dishes of every colour imaginable. And in the middle, a trained octopus held up eight bowls of different dips in its tentacles.

'Whaddyathink?' cried Dudley, suddenly appearing at her side.

'Food as theatre,' replied Delicia, shivering with delight. 'I especially like the octopus.'

Dudley capered about the room. 'He's my favourite, too!'

Next door, there was a sound of people laughing and talking. 'Did you sort out those dreadful children?' asked Delicia.

'They're safe until it's time for them to appear,' replied Dudley, tickling the octopus under the chin. 'By then we'll have all the evidence Aunt Tabitha needs to put these scoundrels in jail.'

'Jail's too good for 'em,' cried Delicia. 'I'd have them whipped and dunked, then—'

Dudley put his finger on his wife's silver lips. 'Hush, my precious antique. Things have changed since our day.'

'Huh,' muttered Delicia. 'Cheats and liars never change.'

* * *

'There's something funny going on here,' said Eddy Swipe out of the side of his mouth.

'Don't be daft,' hissed Cynthia. 'Did you telephone Gordon?'

Eddy nodded. 'He's going to meet us in the maze after we pay those kids off.'

'Is he bringing the papers for the old lady to sign?'

Eddy nodded but his mind was elsewhere. He hadn't noticed the pig pen when he'd first looked around the castle, but he would never forget the two pigs he had seen on his way to his room. They were running back and forth behind the wooden stakes, squealing at the tops of their voices. It was almost as if they were trying to tell him something. Normally Eddy would never have thought like this. He had no imagination and didn't want one. But there was something in the two little pigs' eyes that made him feel sure he had met them before. Don't be stupid, he told himself. How can you meet a pig?

He looked up at the front of Quagmire Castle and tried to picture all the baths overflowing and the water running down the walls and the ceilings falling in. Anything to take his mind away from the look in those little pigs' eyes.

There was a tinkle of a silver spoon on a crystal glass. On the far side of the lawn, Aunt Tabitha climbed on to a little box.

Cynthia looked around quickly. 'Everyone's got a glass except us,' she hissed.

'Compliments of the house,' said a voice at her shoulder. Delicia held out a tray with two green triangular cocktail glasses. She was dressed in her best waitress's outfit with a headdress of pearls and sequins and black feathers.

'What is it?' asked Cynthia, sniffing at the glass.

'My own speciality,' replied Delicia, fixing her with her sapphire eyes.

'About time, too,' said Eddy rudely and grabbed a glass in his hands.

'Ladies and gentlemen,' cried Aunt Tabitha. 'I would like to take this opportunity to welcome you all to Quagmire Castle Country House Hotel! May I wish you a pleasant stay and do please tell all your friends about us.' She held up her glass. 'To Quagmire Castle!'

'To fifty bungalows!' muttered Eddy. He winked at Cynthia and gulped his cocktail in one. It was the strangest stuff he had ever tasted.

Beside him, Cynthia swallowed her own cocktail and looked puzzled. If she hadn't known better, and of course, she always knew best, Cynthia could have sworn the liquid in her glass tasted like toadspawn. Or at least how she imagined toadspawn might taste.

'Seconds?' cried Delicia holding up a green bottle. Cynthia stared. It looked just like the bottle the waiter with the curly hair was tipping into the other guests' glasses across the lawn and they all seemed to be having more. Idiots, she told herself. No taste.

She tipped out the remains of her glass and threw it in to the bushes. 'I'll wait for the banquet.'

'Excellent!' replied Delicia. She grinned wolfishly. 'You won't be disappointed!'

Across the lawn, Herbert Flubber helped Aunt Tabitha down from her box. 'How did I sound?' she asked.

'You were wonderful, Aunt,' said Emily quickly. As she spoke, she looked around at the crowd of people. Everyone was there except Trixie and Norman. A nasty clammy feeling fluttered across her stomach as she caught a smug smile on Cynthia's Swipe's face.

'Jack,' she whispered. 'Where are—'

'I've looked everywhere,' replied Jack in an edgy voice.

'What are we going to do?' said Emily.

'What are we going to do?' cried Aunt Tabitha gaily. 'We're going to have dinner.' She turned and pointed to where a huge dinner gong was set out on the grass. 'Herbert! Ring the gong! The banquet will begin!'

Just as the gong rang out, a beaten-up van roared up the drive and screeched to a halt outside the front door.

Everyone watched as a tubby little man, dressed in a black and white stripy sweater with a mask over his face, jumped out of the van. He pulled off the mask and walked quickly over the lawn to where Aunt Tabitha was standing. 'Good day to you, dear lady,' he cried. He held out his hand. 'Miss Tabitha Quagmire, I presume.' He took Aunt Tabitha's hand and kissed it. 'Allow me to introduce myself. The name's Dosh. Reggie Dosh.' He flashed a sparkling white smile. 'May I intrude on your time a moment?'

Even though Aunt Tabitha wasn't used to such odd goings-on, she found herself rather taken by this strange little man. What's more, no one had kissed her hand for as long as she could remember. 'Of course you may!' An exciting idea popped into Aunt Tabitha's head. 'As long as you join us for dinner.'

'How very kind,' cried Reggie Dosh. He looked over his shoulder at two raccoon faces peering out of the back window of the van. 'Would you mind if my associates came along, too?' He waved his arm and two little men with sweet smiles pulled off their masks and jumped out. 'You see, we're making this, uh, film about honest burglars,' explained Reggie Dosh. 'It's the story of this loveable little guy who rightfully re-acquires money that was wrongfully taken from him by a nasty husband-and-wife team. After which he goes into the world to start a new life!' Reggie Dosh threw back his head and laughed. 'I love happy endings!'

'How splendid!' cried Aunt Tabitha. 'So do I!'

The sun sparkled on something gold and Reggie Dosh found himself looking at Eddy Swipe's front tooth. It was a front tooth he knew well and didn't like one little bit. A wide smile spread on Reggie Dosh's face. Because even though he didn't believe in magic, there was something extraordinary about this place. He was beginning to think there was a reason why his beaten-up van had suddenly developed a mind of its own and lurched down the drive to Quagmire Castle.

Reggie Dosh took Aunt Tabitha by the arm and walked towards the front door. It must mean the moment had come to sort out some unfinished business with Cynthia and Eddy Swipe!

* * *

Damian Sponge and Velveteen Gray stared at each other over the single candle that floated in a bowl of pondweed and buttercups. Usually, Velveteen Gray prided herself on ordering the most complicated dish on the menu and then informing the waiter at the last minute that she was a strict vegetarian. It was her clever way of assessing the correct star rating for the hotels and restaurants she inspected. But tonight it was different. Her stuffed swan and raw salmon slices were delicious and perfectly suited to the dish of stewed pigs' ears that accompanied them. She'd even eaten the candied beetroot on a stick that had arrived for pudding. Damian was amazed. For the first time, there was colour in Velveteen's cheeks and for the first time, he noticed that she was really rather pretty.

'Damian,' whispered Velveteen Gray. 'Have I ever told you how much I like your car?'

'Gosh,' cried Damian, suddenly tingling with delight. 'Gosh! I say! Do you? Do you really?'

* * *

'Gordon *who*?' asked Reggie Dosh. Now he was convinced there was something extraordinary about this place. Now he knew why his van had roared down the drive. He looked at Jack's serious face and put down his knife and fork.

'Gordon Grabbit,' explained Jack. 'He's Aunt Tabitha's bank manager.'

Reggie's Dosh's round face turned thoughtful as he watched Aunt Tabitha laughing and talking to Sybil and Simon Breadsop on the other side of the room.

'Do you know him?' asked Emily quickly.

'I certainly do,' said Reggie Dosh. He lowered his voice. 'And he wasn't a bank manager when I met him.'

Jack and Emily exchanged looks. From the moment they had first met this funny little man, they had both liked him enormously. They felt they could trust him. They took a deep breath and told Reggie all they knew about Gordon Grabbit and Cynthia and Eddy Swipe.

* * *

Cynthia Swipe fiddled with the food on her plate and glared at her husband.

'What's wrong?' said Eddy with his mouth full. 'The food's free.' He drained his glass. 'Anyway, we'll be out of here any minute now.'

'Something's gone wrong, Eddy,' said Cynthia, in a hoarse voice. She had a heavy lumpy feeling in her stomach and she didn't like it. 'I can feel it.'

'You're just looking for trouble,' said Eddy, spraying bits of suckling pig all over the table. He put down the bone he was chewing. 'Look, if it makes you feel any better, we'll leave now, pay off those brats early and meet up with Gordon in the maze.'

He turned to where Aunt Tabitha was talking earnestly to Reggie Dosh. 'It won't make any difference to the old lady when she signs the papers so it might as well be sooner than later.'

They pushed back their chairs and were about to get up when Delicia leapt into the middle of the room and jingled a teaspoon against a glass.

The room fell silent.

'Ladies and gentlemen,' she cried. 'We hope you enjoyed your banquet at Quagmire Castle.'

There was a round of applause and Damian Sponge said, 'Hear. Hear.'

'Marvellous!' cried Delicia. She spun round and pointed to a pair of red velvet curtains that hung across the far end of the room. Everyone stared. It was amazing! No one had noticed them until that minute!

Delicia grinned at the astonished faces in front of her and laughed a deep throaty laugh. 'To enrich your evening's pleasure, we have a little entertainment for you.' Delicia stared deep into Cynthia and Eddy Swipe's eyes. 'I believe you will find it changes your lives for ever.'

A cold sick feeling gripped Eddy for the first time. How could he have been so stupid? Cynthia was right. Cynthia was always right. Something was going to happen to them. And it was something bad. 'Let's get out of here now,' he muttered.

But it was too late. The lights went down and the curtains went up. Cynthia thought she was going to be sick. There was Gordon Grabbit standing in what looked like the middle of the maze. In one hand, he held a thick brown envelope. In the other, he held a torch. The strange thing was that he seemed to have no idea that he was in a room full of people.

'Cynthia! Eddy!' Gordon Grabbit flashed the torch around the room. 'Where are you?' The torch beam caught Cynthia full in the face. She shielded her eyes against its lights.

'Gordon,' she snarled. 'Shuddup and stop making a fool of yourself?'

But Gordon appeared not to hear her. 'Have you trashed the place yet?' he asked in an urgent voice. 'I've got the papers for the old lady to sign.'

'We don't know what you're talking about,' snarled Eddy, looking desperately around for a way out.

'Oh yes, you do,' boomed Dudley Nightshade.

* * *

Two spotlights swept across the room and stopped to reveal Trixie and Norman standing together on the stage. They weren't pigs anymore and they weren't pasty-faced, nasty-looking children, either. In fact, they looked so different, for a moment neither of their parents recognised them.

'We have an announcement to make,' said Norman.

'And we're very, very ashamed of ourselves,' said Trixie.

And without further ado, they told everyone in the room how they had tried to flood the hotel and cause as much damage as they possibly could.

Dudley stepped onto the stage. 'And why did you do this?'

Trixie and Norman lifted their arms and pointed across the room. 'Because Cynthia and Eddy Swipe promised to pay us lots of money.'

You could have heard a champagne bubble pop. The room went silent and everyone stared as the two spotlights flew over the tables and stopped where Cynthia and Eddy and Gordon Grabbit were now standing and glaring at each other.

'It was Gordon's idea,' shrieked Cynthia. 'He cheated the old lady to make her sell up.'

Gordon Grabbit looked around him. It was as if a spell had suddenly been broken. Here was his sister trying to blame everything on him again! Well, this time, Gordon wasn't going to have it!

'It was *your* idea,' he snarled. 'And I've got the letter to prove it!' He put down the torch and pulled a bright pink envelope out of his pocket. 'On your special headed notepaper!'

'Goodness gracious,' murmured Aunt Tabitha who was convinced she was watching a play. 'What scoundrels! The poor old lady! Is there anything we can do to help?'

Reggie Dosh's bright eyes twinkled in the candlelight. 'Leave it to me.' And quick as a flash, he leapt across the room, snatched the two envelopes that Gordon Grabbit was waving in the air. At the same time, his two associates placed themselves firmly behind Gordon Grabbit and Eddy and Cynthia Swipe and marched them out of the room.

'Bravo!' cried Delicia. 'Let the music begin!'

Out of nowhere, the sound of violins filled the air and if Jack and Emily hadn't been listening extra carefully they would never have heard the high wail of the police sirens outside.

'Will you dance with me, my darling?' It was

Damian Sponge's voice but it was a voice he had never heard before.

Velveteen Gray smiled shyly and allowed herself to be led on to the floor. Beside them Sybil and Simon Breadsop were holding hands with Nick and Trixie. And in the middle, laughing like children themselves, Reggie Dosh spun round and round with Aunt Tabitha clasped in his arms.

Jack and Emily sat back on their chairs and stared around at the glittering room. Dudley and Delicia were nowhere to be seen.

* * *

'Jack! Emily!'

It was the next morning and Aunt Tabitha's voice sounded high and excited.

Jack and Emily ran downstairs to see her holding an enormous golden reception bell. 'It's from the hotel inspectors,' she cried. 'It's the highest award a hotel can win!'

Before Jack or Emily had time to speak, there was a knock on the door and the postman handed Aunt Tabitha an important-looking white envelope. She ripped it open, gasped and sat down on the chair.

'Is something the matter?' cried Jack.

'I don't believe it!' cried Aunt Tabitha. She looked down at the paper. 'The bank has cancelled my debts and given me back the deeds to Quagmire Castle.' Aunt Tabitha shook her hand in amazement. 'Not only that, they've given me back all the money I've ever paid them.'

'Quite right, too!' said a voice. Reggie Dosh appeared at the door. 'We can't have crooks like Gordon Grabbit and those Swipes buzzing about like nasty fat flies.' He grinned at Aunt Tabitha. 'And talking about flying,' – he held up a set of goggles and a long purple scarf – 'would you come with me in my aeroplane. I bought it specially this morning.'

'Why, I'd delighted to, Mr Dosh,' cried Aunt Tabitha. 'How did you know I loved flying?' She wrapped the scarf around her neck. 'And purple is absolutely my favourite colour.' Suddenly her face went serious. 'But the hotel. Perhaps—'

'We'll look after the hotel, Aunt Tabitha,' said Emily quickly.

'Are you sure, dears?'

'Absolutely sure,' said Jack. 'Mrs Gristle is almost better and Mr Flubber will help.'

Aunt Tabitha still looked worried. 'What about those two lovely people?' She shook her head. 'I never thanked them and they just disappeared.'

Emily laughed. 'They'll be around if we need them, Aunt Tabitha.'

Five minutes later, Jack and Emily watched as Reggie Dosh handed Aunt Tabitha into a shiny red seaplane that bobbed gently on Toadspawn Lake. They had never seen their aunt look so happy. 'Byeeee!' she cried. 'Byeee!' She blew them a kiss and the seaplane's engines started up with a throaty roar.

* * *

Jack and Emily walked up the front steps of Quagmire Castle and stood in the hall. All the guests had gone. Even the Breadsops had decided to leave because Norman and Trixie needed to get home and pack before they went away to camp.

'Whew!' said Jack, falling back in an armchair and letting his legs swing over the side. 'What an adventure!' He turned to where Emily was staring at the wall at the far end of the hallway. 'Do you know, I worked out that Delicia and Dudley are probably our great-great-great-great-great-grandparents?'

Emily burst out laughing. 'Jack!' she cried. 'Look at the portraits!'

Jack turned and burst out laughing, too.

Across the wall, Delicia and Dudley stared out of the portraits. They were grinning and Powderball was pulling a really stupid face!

ABOUT THE AUTHOR

Karen Wallace was born in Canada and grew up in a log cabin in the backwoods of Quebec. She spent her early days messing about on the river, climbing trees and building toboggan runs in winter.

Karen settled in England in 1982 with her husband and two small sons. Since then she has had various jobs including singing cabaret, running a regional publishing company and making pizzas.

She began writing for children full time in 1991. Her fervent hope is that, while growing old gracefully, she may never grow up.

Karen has had over eighty books published. For A&C Black these include *Something Slimy on Primrose Drive; Yikes, it's a Yeti!; Aargh, it's an Alien!* and the *Crook Catchers* series. Her novel *Raspberries on the Yangtze* was shortlisted for the *Guardian* Children's Fiction Prize in 2001. She has also written numerous scripts for children's television.

'Many years ago I read a story by Oscar Wilde called *The Canterville Ghost*. It was the first time I had read a ghost story that was funny and eventually I dreamed up Dudley and Delicia Nightshade and another ancestral home called Quagmire Castle.'

Another fantastic Black Cat ...

KAREN WALLACE
Something Slimy on Primrose Drive

Life on Primrose Drive will never be the same again! The Wolfbane family have moved into No. 34. They've soon changed the swimming pool into a swamp and transformed the kitchen into a dungeon.

Next door, the Rigid-Smythe family are horrified by the new arrivals. However when a devious conman steals all their savings, the Rigid-Smythes turn to their new neighbours for help. Can the two families overcome their differences to defeat his sinister scheming?

Another fantastic Black Cat ...

ELIZABETH ARNOLD
The Gold-Spectre

Everything about the wild Scottish
countryside seems unpredictable to
city boy Joe – even his new best
friend, Robbie. But the two boys must
trust each other when they try to
put right a crime from the distant
past, and face an angry ghost
protecting a hoard of stolen gold ...

Another fantastic Black Cat ...

REBECCA LISLE
Planimal Magic

Joe is staying with his cousins in the
country where his uncle runs a scientific
research institute. Late at night there's a
terrible, heart-stopping wail coming from
outside. Who – or what – is making it?

When Joe, his psychic dog, Bingo,
and cousin, Molly, embark on a search,
they make a magical, mysterious
discovery which some people will do
anything to keep secret ...

Black Cats – collect them all!

The Gold-Spectre • Elizabeth Arnold
The Ramsbottom Rumble • Georgia Byng
Calamity Kate • Terry Deary
The Custard Kid • Terry Deary
Footsteps in the Fog • Terry Deary
The Ghosts of Batwing Castle • Terry Deary
Ghost Town • Terry Deary
Into the Lion's Den • Terry Deary
The Joke Factory • Terry Deary
The Treasure of Crazy Horse • Terry Deary
The Wishing Well Ghost • Terry Deary
A Witch in Time • Terry Deary
Planimal Magic • Rebecca Lisle
Eyes Wide Open • Jan Mark
Dear Ms • Joan Poulson
Spook School • Sue Purkiss
It's a Tough Life • Jeremy Strong
Big Iggy • Kaye Umansky
Quirky Times at Quagmire Castle • Karen Wallace
Something Slimy on Primrose Drive • Karen Wallace
Drucilla and the Cracked Pot • Lynda Waterhouse
Moonmallow Smoothie • Philip Wooderson